The Very Very Very Long Dog

Written and illustrated by
Julia Patton

sourcebooks jabberwocky

Cover design by Sourcebooks

Pencil, crayon, oil paint, and digital techniques were used to create the full color art.

Published by Sourcebooks, Inc.
P.O. Box 4410, Naperville, Illinois 60567-4410
(630) 961-3900
Fax: (630) 961-2168
sourcebooks.com

Library of Congress Cataloging-in-Publication Data is on file with the publisher.

Source of Production: Leo Paper, Heshan City, Guangdong Province, China
Date of Production: August 2017
Run Number: 5010038

Printed and bound in China.
LEO 10 9 8 7 6 5 4 3 2 1

BARTELBY'S BOTTOM →

This is Bartelby.

Well, this is his bottom, anyway.

HERE IS HIS FRONT END! ↓
heLLo
* Waving

Bartelby is a very very very long sausage dog who's lucky enough to live in this beautiful old bookstore.

Every day Bartelby eats breakfast whilst reading his favorite books.

Then his special friends take him for his morning walk around town.

Bartelby loves his home, his walks, and his friends.

Life couldn't be any better!

Except Bartelby is SO long, he's not always quite sure where his bottom is.

His walks started out great...

BUS

But unfortunately didn't always end so well. His friends tried their very best to help clean up the mess.

Bartelby had no idea.

OPEN
90% OFF
HATS
FOR RENT
FOR RENT
TAXI

Day after day, they carefully trotted across Main Street.

But his blundering backside caused a calamity!

Oh, Bartelby!
TAXI
Beep!
Yikes! sorry!

STOP
Wet cement
CEMENT
CEMENT
CEMEN
mum
Pat
Pat

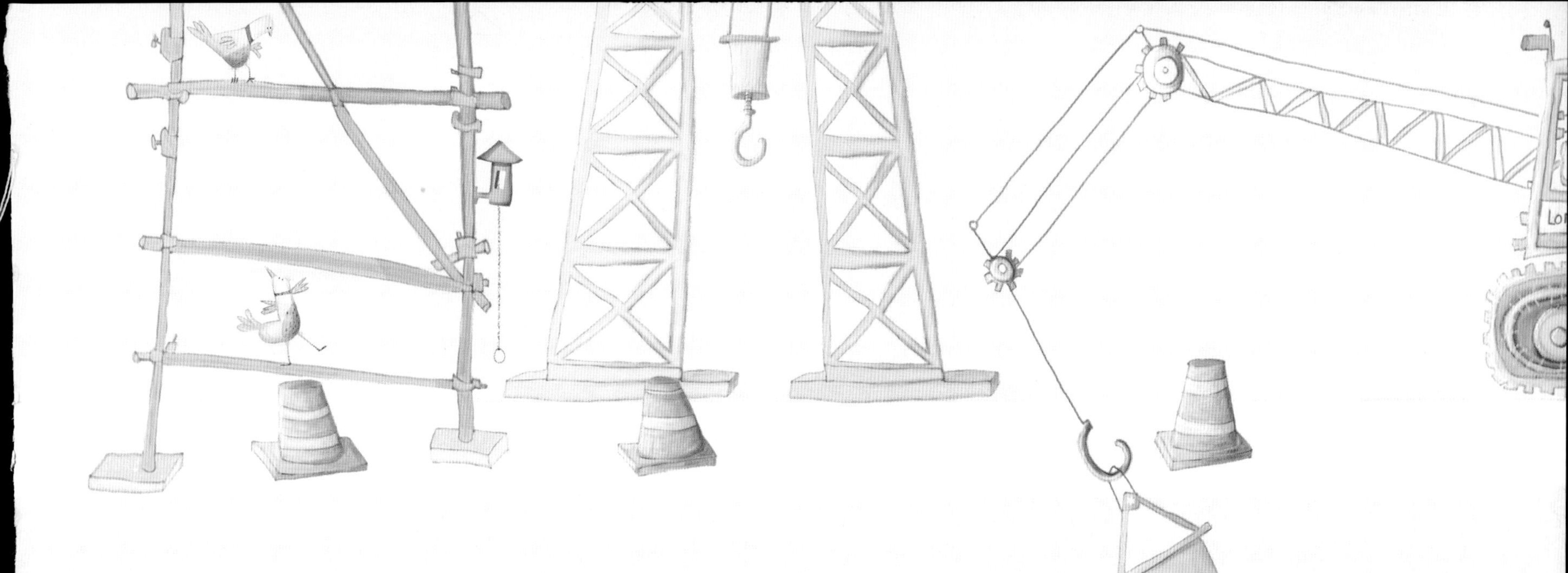

They cautiously took a diversion around the construction site.

But his bungling behind created even more chaos!

Oh, Bartelby!
OH MY!
WE'RE TERRIBLY SORRY!

One day, Bartelby's reckless rear made so much mayhem that not even his friends could fix it this time.

Oh, Bartelby!

sorry, Sir!
Oh no!

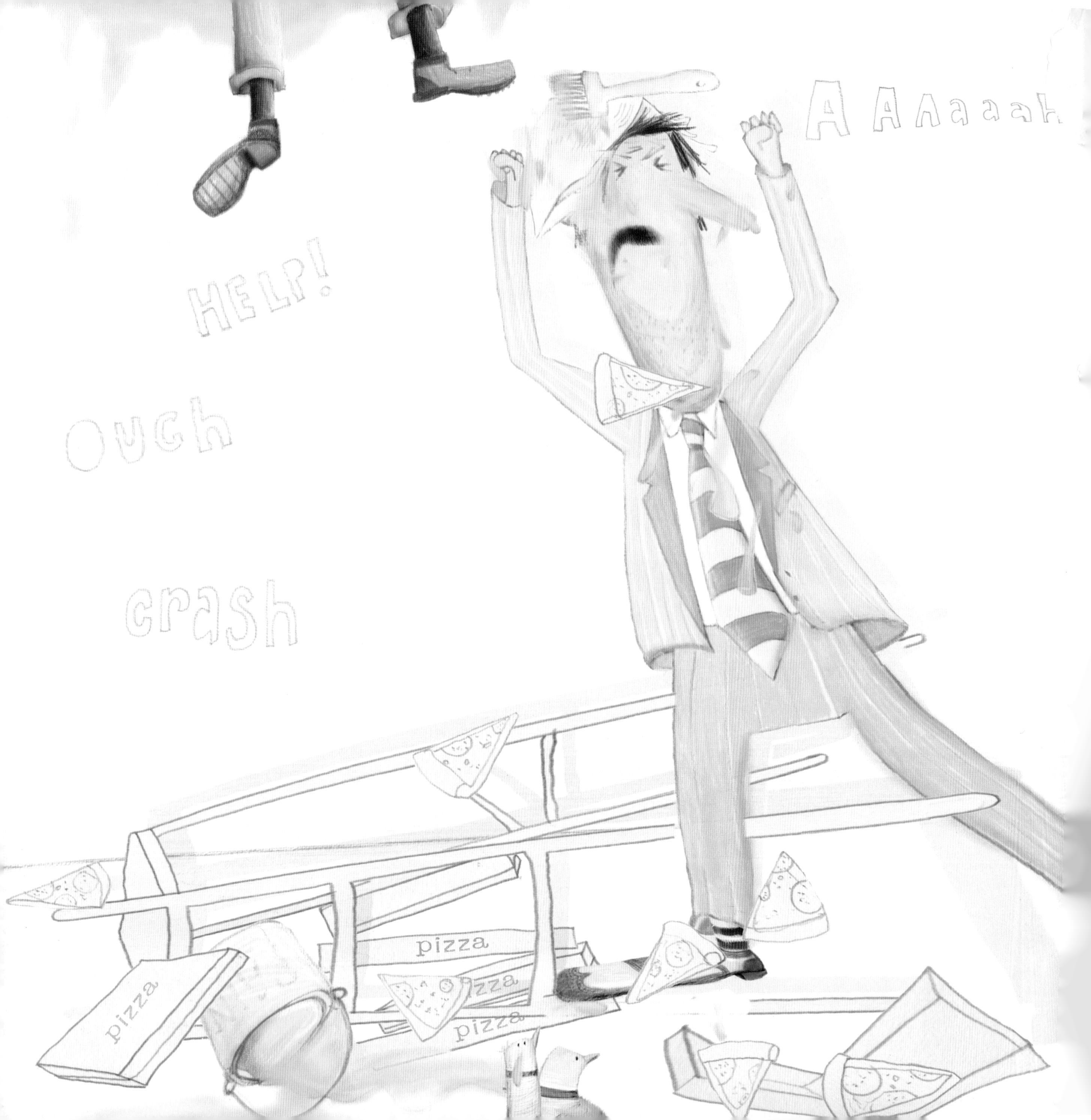
AAAaaaah
HELP!
Ouch
crash
pizza
pizza
pizza
pizza

Bartelby heard yelling and shouting, and turned back to investigate.

He would get to the bottom of this and find the culprit!

Grrrrrr!

Poor Bartelby realized that it was his very own bottom that had caused all the crashing and bashing, making everyone unhappy.

He ran all the way home and was so sad he didn't even read his favorite bedtime story. (He still ate his dinner.)

He vowed never to leave the bookstore again.

Bartelby's friends were heartbroken to see him so sad. They loved him just the way he was. They rummaged through all the bookshelves searching for answers.

They concocted a most marvelous plan that just might make Bartelby feel better. They created a very special gift—a gift for Bartelby to help himself.

Every day, Bartelby still eats breakfast whilst reading his favorite books.

His special friends still take him for his morning walk around town.

But now Bartelby is absolutely sure where his bottom is!

Oh,
Bartelby!
GO
HAT
PRESS
SALE
TODAY
SEEDS
pizza
pizza
pizza
pizza
pizza
pizza
TAXI
LONG VEHICLE

BUS
LIBRARY